CLAIRE SCHUMACHER

KING OF THE
ZOO

WILLIAM MORROW & COMPANY · NEW YORK

Library of Congress Cataloging in Publication Data
Schumacher, Claire.   King of the zoo.
Summary: The naughty, but good-hearted, zoo animals play a joke on
their keeper, the "King of the Zoo."   1. Children's stories, American.
[1. Zoo animals—Fiction] I. Title. PZ7.S3914Ki 1985 [E] 84-1099
ISBN 0-688-04131-0
ISBN 0-688-04132-9 (lib. bdg.)

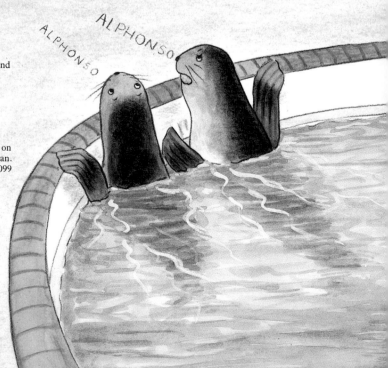

Alphonso is proud of his tidy zoo.

"Good morning, seals. Good morning to you."
"Phooey, Alphonso. Phooey on you.
    Did you clean our pool? We want a balloon.
    Do you have our fish? Quick—or we'll splash,"
bark Jessica, Rebecca, and Ophelia.

And that is what they did.

"Good morning, Eloise. Good morning, Leonard."
"You're almost late," trumpets Eloise.
"Is that all you have?" growls Leonard.
"We want cookies. We want peanuts. We want toys."

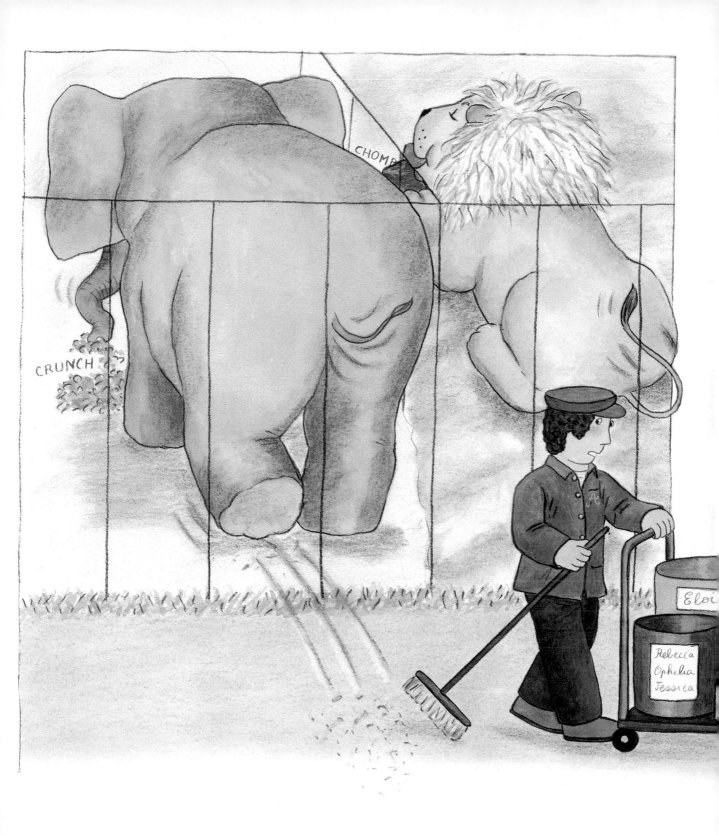

"I've given you so much already," says Alphonso.
But Eloise and Leonard aren't listening.

"Hello, Mambo, Tom-Tom, and Bamboo. Hello,
Takko and Rokko. Look what I have for you."
"Oh, no. Not bananas!" shriek the monkeys.
"Birdseed *again*?" screech the parrots.

"But, my dear little monkeys and parrots,
   I want you to be strong and healthy."
"No, Alphonso. We want candy. We want ice cream.
   We want everything the children have."

"Be quiet, please," says Alphonso.
"It's time to open the gate."

"Welcome to the zoo.
Enjoy your visit.
I'm Alphonso,
the zookeeper."

But no sooner is the gate opened when…

"Stop it, Jessica! Ophelia!
Give the boy back his ball."

CLICK

"Shhhh, Leonard. You are scaring our visitors."
"Humph!" pouts Leonard. "I'm not even
    allowed to clear my throat."

"Look out, Alphonso!" shriek Takko and Rokko.
"It's raining seeds."

A man tries to get the monkeys to make funny faces.

But everyone laughs at *him*.

"They mean no harm," Alphonso says.
"They like to play...like children do."

"Oh, my, what a day," Alphonso sighs as he shuts the gate. "Those naughties have worn me out." But Alphonso has forgotten to do something inside the zoo.

He's forgotten to lock the monkeys' cage.

The animals laugh and play all night long.
They have tired cheeks from so much laughing,
and their eyes are starting to close. It's almost
time to begin the day again. But there is still
time to fool Alphonso.

When the zookeeper opens the gate, the cages are empty. "What a disaster," gasps Alphonso. "My little darlings have disappeared!"

"SURPRISE!"

"Oh, how awful," cries Alphonso.
"I thought you all ran away,
   and I would never see you again."

"Alphonso, don't cry. It was only a joke."

"Don't worry, Alphonso.
We'll try to be good. We'll clean up the zoo.
You'll be amazed at what we can do."